Farmer John's Big Lesson: In Community

Farmer John's Big Lesson:
In Community

written by

Detreich Fluellen

MYND MATTERS

MYND MATTERS PUBLISHING

715 PEACHTREE STREET NE

SUITES 100 & 200

ATLANTA, GA 30308

WWW.MYNDMATTERSPUBLISHING.COM

ISBN: 978-1-953307-43-9 (PBK)

ISBN: 978-1-953307-42-2 (HDCV)

FIRST EDITION

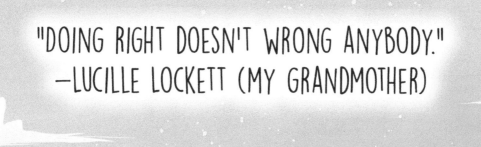

"DOING RIGHT DOESN'T WRONG ANYBODY."
—LUCILLE LOCKETT (MY GRANDMOTHER)

ONCE UPON A GEORGIA VALLEY,
NEAR THE MIDDLE OF THE STATE,
LIVED A MAN, HARDWORKING AND HAPPY,
FARMER JOHN WAS HIS NAME.

EVERY MORNING HE WOKE BEFORE THE SUN,
TO FEED HIS ANIMALS AND TEND HIS LAND.
ALWAYS COMMITTED TO DOING THE WORK,
EVEN WITH WORN FEET AND ROUGH HANDS.

HE WALKED THE FIELD AND GATHERED FALLEN SEEDS,
SINGING TO HIMSELF AS HE WENT.
HE FILLED HIS BUCKETS UNTIL THEY OVERFLOWED,
HOPING THE SEEDS WOULD SERVE OTHERS' BENEFIT.

12

OFF TO TOWN HE WENT EACH WEEK,
TO MEET WITH FRIENDS AND SHOP FOR GOODS.
FROM CHEFS AND FLORISTS TO DOCTORS AND TEACHERS,
FARMER JOHN SPOKE WITH EVERYONE HE COULD.

HE'D SHARE A KIND WORD OR TWO OR THREE,
AND BEFORE THEY'D PART, GIVE A HANDFUL OF SEEDS.
HIS REMINDER TO ALL WAS PLAIN AND CLEAR,
YOUR CHARACTER IS SHOWN IN EVERY DEED.

ONE DAY HE RETURNED FROM ONE OF HIS TRIPS,
READY TO TILL THE SOIL AND PUT THINGS IN ORDER.
BUT HE SAW A FIRE BLAZING ACROSS HIS FARM,
AND FIREFIGHTERS BLASTING LONG HOSES OF WATER.

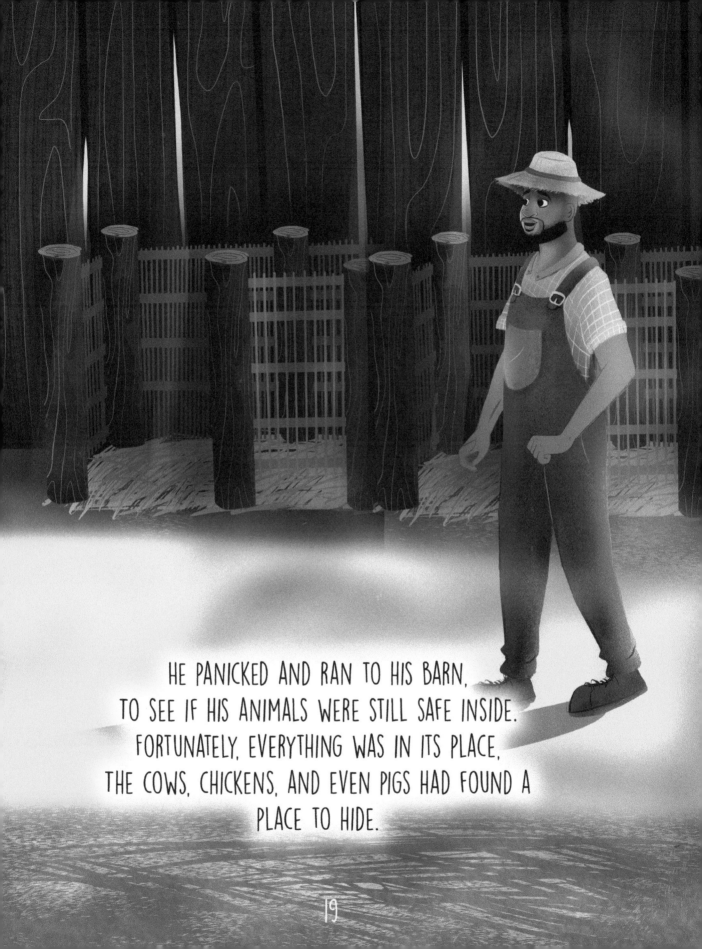

HE PANICKED AND RAN TO HIS BARN,
TO SEE IF HIS ANIMALS WERE STILL SAFE INSIDE.
FORTUNATELY, EVERYTHING WAS IN ITS PLACE,
THE COWS, CHICKENS, AND EVEN PIGS HAD FOUND A
PLACE TO HIDE.

FARMER JOHN WALKED OUTSIDE AND FELL TO HIS KNEES,
PAINED BY WHAT HIS EYES DID SEE.
MOST OF HIS FARM WAS BURNED BY THE FIRE,
HIS YEARS OF HARD WORK, ONLY A MEMORY.

WHAT WILL I DO NOW? HE THOUGHT TO HIMSELF
AS HE WANDERED AROUND FEELING LOST.
BUT LITTLE DID HE KNOW, HIS GOOD DEEDS OF OLD
WERE SOON ABOUT TO PAY OFF.

AS HE SAT IN HIS ROOM WITH HIS HEAD HUNG LOW,
FEELING QUITE SAD AND ALONE,
HE HEARD A KNOCK AT THE DOOR AND THEN CAME TO FIND,
ALL OF HIS FRIENDS SURROUNDING HIS HOME.

THEY'D HEARD WHAT HAPPENED AND RUSHED TO HELP
FARMER JOHN DEAL WITH HIS TRAGEDY.
THEY WANTED TO SHOW HIM, HE WASN'T ALONE,
HE HAD A LOVING AND SUPPORTIVE COMMUNITY.

THEY STOOD WITH SHOVELS AND BUCKETS OF SEEDS,
READY TO REPLACE WHAT WAS LOST.

THEY BROUGHT EVERYTHING FARMER JOHN
COULD POSSIBLY NEED,
AND HE DIDN'T HAVE TO WORRY
ABOUT THE COST.

OVERWHELMED WITH GRATITUDE
HIS EYES WELLED WITH TEARS,
HOW COULD HE POSSIBLY REPAY THE DEBT.
THEY'D SHOWN SUCH LOVE AND GENEROSITY
OF WHICH HE WOULD NEVER FORGET.

AS PEOPLE CONTINUED TO GATHER AROUND,
COMING FROM NEAR AND FAR.
FARMER JOHN GAZED OUT OVER THE CROWD
AND FELT A STRONG TUG ON HIS HEART.

HE NOW KNEW HE WAS NEVER ALONE,
HIS FRIENDS WERE ALWAYS AROUND.
HE HUGGED EACH ONE AND STARTED TO SING,
THANKFUL FOR THE LOVE HE'D FOUND.

WORKING TOGETHER, THEY TILLED THE LAND,
ENSURING NO DAMAGE REMAINED.
THEY PLANTED NEW SEEDS IN FERTILE SOIL.
AND THERE, A NEW CROP BECAME.

FARMER JOHN STILL GOES TO TOWN EACH WEEK
OFFERING EVEN MORE SMILES AND SEEDS.
HE SHARES HIS WISDOM, WORDS, AND ABUNDANT WEALTH,
WITH OTHERS WHO MAY FIND THEMSELVES IN NEED.

HE URGES ALL TO BE KIND, GIVING, AND TRUE,
TO LIVE BY A RIGHTEOUS CREED.
FARMER JOHN'S WORDS REMIND ALL WHO SEEK,
YOUR CHARACTER IS SHOWN IN EVERY DEED!

CPSIA information can be obtained
at www.ICGtesting.com
Printed in the USA
LVHW071119030221
678222LV00007B/784

9 781953 307439